WELCOME TO

Collect the special coins in this book.
You will earn one gold coin for
every chapter you read.

Once you have finished all the chapters,
find out what to do with your gold coins at
the back of the book.

With special thanks to Tabitha Jones

For Sebastian and Dominic Fairhead

www.beastquest.co.uk

ORCHARD BOOKS
338 Euston Road, London NW1 3BH
Orchard Books Australia
Level 17/207 Kent St, Sydney, NSW 2000

A Paperback Original
First published in Great Britain in 2015

Beast Quest is a registered trademark of Beast Quest Limited
Series created by Beast Quest Limited, London

Text © Beast Quest Limited 2015
Cover and inside illustrations by Steve Sims
© Beast Quest Limited 2015

A CIP catalogue record for this book is available from
the British Library.

ISBN 978 1 40833 489 8

1 3 5 7 9 10 8 6 4 2

Printed and bound by CPI Group (UK) Ltd, Croydon, CR0 4YY

The paper and board used in this book are made from wood
from responsible sources.

Orchard Books is an imprint of Hachette Children's Group
and published by The Watts Publishing Group Limited,
an Hachette UK company.

www.hachette.co.uk

Xerik
THE BONE CRUNCHER

BY ADAM BLADE

ORCHARD

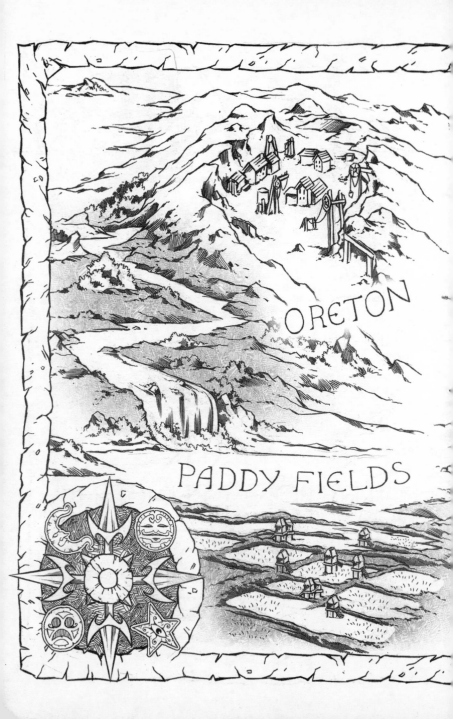

ORETON

PADDY FIELDS

CONTENTS

Dear Reader

You join us at a moment of great historical importance. King Hugo of Avantia is about to make an official visit to our neighbours in the south, the kingdom of Tangala. Tangala was once Avantia's staunchest ally, but the kingdoms have been at odds for decades. Now, the marriage of His Majesty to Tangala's Queen Aroha will unite our kingdoms once again.

Tangala is the only kingdom in which no Beasts lurk. Powerful ancient magic protects the kingdom's borders from Evil. It is our hope that this journey should be a simple one, untouched by danger...

But things are rarely so simple.

Aduro
Former Wizard to King Hugo

PROLOGUE

Brennan shoved his hands deeper into his pockets and frowned into the wind. It scoured the paddy fields of Tangala, sending ripples through the knee-high rice plants sticking out of the shallow water. Swollen black clouds were piled high across the horizon. *I need to hurry if I'm going to beat the storm*, Brennan thought. He gripped the ring in his pocket.

But, first, one more look...

He turned his back to the wind and drew out the ring. It was gold, flecked with shimmering green. *Worth a pretty penny*, Brennan thought. He closed his hand and squinted through the swirling mist curling around him like fingers. As far as he could tell, the fields were empty. Brennan chuckled at his own fear. *No one's going to steal it. Even the old fool that gave it to me will be sheltering somewhere out of this weather.*

But thinking of the stranger he'd met earlier made Brennan feel uneasy and he tucked the ring away. The man had risen suddenly from the roadside, his face as lined and weather-browned as a vagrant's. But then Brennan had noticed the man's dark eyes. They were cold and flinty. Not like a vagrant at all. More like an ex-soldier, or a bandit. "I've no money," Brennan had told him.

"I've got an opportunity for you," the stranger had said. "Take this ring to market and sell it for me, and I'll give you half the profits. Meet me back here in two days' time."

Brennan had agreed, half out of fear, but since then he'd made a better plan. He'd sell the ring in Pania, and keep all the money for himself. So now here he was, on the long road out of the village, trudging through the gathering storm.

The light was failing fast, so Brennan quickened his pace. A strange slithering sound made the hair on his arms prickle.

"Gah!" Brennan felt a sharp pain in his ankle and looked down. A dull-green bramble had snagged his foot. He pulled his leg away. Something fat and lithe whipped towards him across the path – a twisting root-like tendril, barbed with curved thorns. And there was another!

"Get away!" Brennan yelped, as they snaked towards his feet. A loud squelching sound came from the field ahead, bringing with it a stench like rotting flesh. He stared, frozen with terror, as a thick stem climbed into the sky. At the head of the stem, far above Brennan's head, bulged a huge, waxy blue flower. Brennan's heart thumped as he tried to make sense of it. *A plant? But how?*

He staggered back. His stomach lurched as he teetered off the path and into the flooded field.

Tendrils grabbed his legs, ripping at his flesh. Brennan toppled and fell. Muddy water filled his eyes and nose. The tip of one root was climbing up his thigh…reaching into his pocket. *The ring!*

Suddenly, all the clutching tendrils whipped away. Brennan scrambled onto his hands and knees.

The ring was glistening at the end of a twisting root, held high in the air. The plant's waxy petals split apart, revealing a wide, curved mouth filled with jagged yellow teeth.

"What are you?" Brennan gasped.

"Your reward for daring to steal
from me!" a voice said behind him.
Brennan looked over his shoulder.
The stranger he'd met on the road
grinned back at him, his eyes glinting
coldly. The man clicked his fingers.

"It's time to feed the Beast!" he cried.

The huge plant-Beast lurched towards Brennan. Roots snapped about his wrists and tugged. Brennan's jaw landed in the mud with a smack. He tried to scream, but dirty water filled his mouth.

Brennan squirmed, trying to escape the biting thorns, but only managed to turn onto his back.

The great blue flower hung above him, grinning horribly. Its teeth snapped apart, showing a gaping throat, and deep inside its maw, several round, bulging eyes. The eyes swivelled towards him.

Brennan put his arms over his head and squeezed his eyes shut, waiting for the Beast to bite.

1

THE QUEEN'S GUARD

The morning sun glanced over the mountains that surrounded the village of Oreton.

Tom shielded his eyes and scanned the battered scene. The houses that Wardok the Sky Terror had damaged cast long, jagged shadows, but villagers were already busy clearing rubble from the streets.

Beside him, Elenna pointed.
"There's Jem," she said. Jem was the
boy Tom had saved from Wardok. He
stood squinting upwards, watching
the village quarrymen mending a
roof that Wardok had destroyed.

Tom and Elenna crossed the road
and went to his side. "You'll be back
to normal in no time," Tom said to
the young boy.

Jem grinned up at Tom. "Teach me
to fight Beasts like you do!" he said.

Tom smiled, glad to see the young
boy hadn't lost his courage.

"I'm afraid we've come to say
goodbye," Tom said. Prince Rotu,
the queen's nephew, had already
left in search of the next Beast. Tom
needed to find it first, or the prince

was likely to get himself killed.

Jem looked disappointed, but then grinned again. "Tell me a story before you go! Are you really Avantia's Master of Beasts?" The boy's eyes shone with excitement.

Tom started to shake his head – they needed to get going. But Elenna nudged him. "I'll get Storm ready," she said.

Tom turned to Jem. "I am the Master of the Beasts in Avantia," he explained. "I'm visiting Tangala with the king, but the evil wizard Velmal has stolen Queen Aroha's magic jewels, which kept your kingdom's Beasts in exile."

Jem stopped smiling for a moment. "That's why Wardok came?" he asked. "Because the Treasures of Tangala are gone?"

Tom nodded. "Velmal has given the jewels to the Beasts to protect. I took the crown from Wardok, but there are three more Beasts I need to defeat before I can return all the magic jewels."

"You'll do it!" Jem said. "You saved us from Wardok. You can do anything!"

I wish I could feel so certain, Tom thought. It wasn't just Beasts he was facing. Velmal had made it look like Tom and Elenna were the thieves of the crown jewels, so they were fugitives as well. Unless they recovered the jewels, the planned marriage between King Hugo and

Queen Aroha was doomed. *And that could mean war,* Tom thought. He let his breath out slowly, forcing himself to stay calm. *While there's blood in my veins, I won't let that happen.*

As he turned towards the stables, he felt a faint vibration running through the ground. From somewhere nearby, Silver let out a low growl.

Tom looked up to see a troop of mounted women hurtling down the rocky road towards the village. The morning sun glinted off their armour and their hair streamed behind them.

Tom dashed towards the stables with Jem at his heels. "Elenna!"

he called. "The Queen's Guard are coming!" Elenna emerged with Storm beside her.

"I need you to take Storm and run," Tom told her.

"But we should stick together," Elenna said.

"They'll run us down if we both

ride Storm," Tom said. "But I've got a plan. I'll meet you on the western road out of town."

Elenna glanced at the approaching soldiers and shook her head. "I can't leave you to face them alone."

Tom could feel the horses' hoofbeats thudding towards them. "You have to trust me!" he said.

Elenna frowned. "All right," she said. "But be careful!" She swung herself up into Storm's saddle, gestured to Silver to follow, then galloped away.

Tom turned to Jem. "I need a favour," he said. "The soldiers over there are after me. I need you to block the road."

Jem gaped up at Tom. "How?"

Tom pointed to the top of a high rocky hill bordering the road out of the village. Crops of large boulders rested midway down the slope. "Even small stones can trigger a landslide, if you choose the right ones to push."

Jem grinned. "Leave it to me!" he said, and scampered away.

The horses' hoofbeats came to a stop. Tom turned. Six armoured women on tall warhorses towered above him. Their hair was braided with strips of leather and long swords hung at their sides.

The eyes of the armoured woman at the head of the group flashed as they met Tom's.

"You are under arrest!" she cried. "You will return the queen's jewels then accompany me to the palace."

Tom shook his head. "I didn't steal them," he said. "An evil wizard called Velmal—"

"Enough!" the woman cried angrily. "Save your excuses for your execution day!"

She launched herself from the saddle, hefted an enormous battle-axe from her horse's side and stormed towards Tom.

Tom glanced at the empty saddle, and saw his chance. Using the power of his magic golden boots, he sprang upwards. The soldier's mouth dropped open as he soared over her head. He landed in her saddle with a jolt. The soldier's horse screamed and bucked, but Tom grabbed its reins. He dug in his heels, and the horse leapt forwards.

"Stop him!" the soldier roared.

Hooves thundered behind Tom as he urged the horse onwards, out of the village and onto the rocky road through the mountains.

He spotted Jem high on the slope and lifted a hand. "Now!" Tom cried, gripping the reins firmly.

A rumbling began to build on the mountainside, and soon a wave of huge boulders came hurtling down the slope. Tom raced past just in time, as the boulders slammed into the road in a roaring crash. His horse reared, then shot forwards as the

blast echoed through the mountains.

Tom slowed the mare to a trot, then glanced behind him. At the top of the slope, Jem was jumping up and down with excitement. The road was completely blocked with broken rock and fallen earth. A great cloud of dust filled the air. Above the rattle of falling stones, Tom could hear the angry shouts of the soldiers. Tom grinned. *That's going to take half a day to clear!*

"Tom! Here!" Tom turned to see Elenna step from the roadside with Silver and Storm.

He pulled his horse to a stop and dropped from the saddle to the ground. "Thank you, friend," he said, patting the horse's rump to send it on its way again.

Elenna raised an eyebrow and nodded towards the landslide of rubble blocking the road. "Now the queen's soldiers will be angrier than ever," she said.

Tom grinned. "Then we'd better

make the most of our head start." He
swung himself into Storm's saddle,
and Elenna leapt up behind him.

"Let's go!" Tom cried. "We've got a
Beast to find!"

A PERILOUS CROSSING

Tom pulled Storm to a stop at a fork in the mountain path.

"Where next?" he asked Elenna.

Elenna unfolded Rotu's enchanted map, and held it up between them. She pointed towards a pulsing patch of light on the parchment.

"According to this, the next jewel isn't far," she said, "but look." She traced a snaking blue line with her finger. "There's a river to cross, and I can't see a bridge."

"You're right," said a grave voice. Tom turned and saw Daltec's magical image floating in the air.

The young wizard's face was pinched with worry.

"Daltec!" Tom said. "How are things at the palace?"

"Not good," Daltec said. "The king's wedding is on hold until we clear your name. There are already calls for all Avantians to be banished, and time is against us. I am risking much by talking to you. The Tangalans don't trust magic."

"We've recovered the crown," Tom said, "and we're tracking the next jewel. But so is Rotu. He knows his kingdom well, and he's seen the map. He's probably far ahead of us by now."

Daltec frowned. "Rotu is the queen's nephew," he said. "I don't need to warn you to be careful around him."

"He's more likely to kill himself trying to tackle Beasts alone," Tom muttered.

"In that case I'll bid you farewell," Daltec said. "The sooner you find the next Beast the better." He raised a hand, and vanished.

"We need to go left," Elenna said. "The river won't be far."

They started off at a gallop with Silver running beside them, but the road soon banked steeply downwards. As Tom slowed Storm to a trot, he could hear the roar of rushing water. "That river sounds like a torrent," he said.

Trees and shrubs grew either side of the road. Silver scouted ahead, nosing through the undergrowth. Suddenly he stopped and turned towards them, his hackles raised.

Tom and Elenna dismounted and led Storm on foot. Where Silver waited, the trees gave way to reveal a wide, raging river, white with rapids and strewn with rocks. The sound of rushing water thundered around them. Storm tossed his head worriedly and snorted.

"We can't cross here," Tom said. "Maybe it's calmer further downstream." He called on the power of his golden helmet, and his view narrowed to a single magnified point. He turned his head, searching the riverbank. A patch of brown caught his attention, and his eyes snapped back for a closer view. It was a hut. A flat raft was moored to a jetty beside it.

"There's a crossing," Tom said.

They continued on foot, leading Storm along the riverbank until they reached the wooden hut. A rope had been strung across the river and was tied to a pulley on one side and a winch on the other. Tom had seen similar arrangements in Avantia. By attaching the raft to the rope, it could be moved across the river using the mechanism.

"Hello there!" Tom called. The door to the hut opened, and a shaggy-haired man peered out.

"We need to cross," Tom said. "How much is the fee?"

The man shuffled his feet, looking uncomfortable. "No fee," he said, then turned quickly away and strode towards the jetty.

Tom and Elenna watched as he winched in the raft.

"I wonder why he's not charging us," Elenna said.

Tom shrugged. "I guess we're due a bit of luck."

"Climb aboard," the ferryman said.

"Come on, Storm," Tom said, leading his horse along the jetty. When they reached the moored raft,

Storm tossed his head and baulked. Tom laid a hand on the stallion's muscular flank.

"I've got you," Tom said. He stepped onto the raft ahead of Storm, feeling the rush of water beneath the planks. He put out a hand to guide the horse on. As Storm's hoof landed on the wooden beams, the raft began to tip. Quickly, Tom shifted his weight to steady the raft, and Elenna guided Storm's back legs on board. Silver leapt on after them.

Tom nodded to the ferryman. The man turned his winch, letting the raft slowly out into the river.

The further they got from the jetty, the faster the river flowed. Rapids slapped against the raft, making it dip and jerk. Soon they were soaked with spray.

Suddenly, the raft stopped. Tom glanced towards the shore. The rope ran taut back to the winch, where the ferryman was tying a knot.

"Hey!" Tom called. "What's going on?" The ferryman looked up at him sorrowfully, then walked away.

"Come back!" Tom shouted. *He's leaving us stranded!*

"Tom, look," Elenna said. She was pointing toward the far bank. Tom followed the line of her finger, and his eyes locked with Rotu's. The prince sat astride his tall brown horse, smiling back at them. Tom felt a rush of anger.

"This Quest is mine," Rotu called. "I'd appreciate it if you'd stop interfering."

Tom swallowed his rage. "We should work together," he called.

Rotu shook his head. "I don't work with thieves," he said. Then he

dismounted and drew a knife from his boot. There was a glint of steel as Rotu lifted his arm.

"No!" Tom cried, but Rotu grinned and brought his arm sharply down, slashing the rope.

RUNNING THE RAPIDS

Everything started moving at once.
The riverbank spun away from
Tom as the raft shot down the river.
Storm snorted and tossed his head,
his hooves skidding on sodden wood.

"Storm, Silver! Lie down!" Tom
shouted over the roar of the rushing
water. He pressed his hands firmly
on the stallion's back. Storm lowered

himself to his knees, then to his side. Silver hunkered down beside him.

Tom glanced towards the shore. Rocks and scrubby trees were whirling past, and Rotu was long out of sight.

"We've got to find a way to stop!" said Tom. He tried reaching for a boulder as they skimmed along, but he couldn't find purchase on the slick, wet rock.

Elenna leaned out over the water and reached for the trailing rope that had tied them to the shore.

Thud! The raft hit a rock and reared upwards. Silver snarled and Storm let out a panicked snort. Tom grabbed hold of Elenna's tunic to keep her from falling into the

torrent. His stomach flipped as the
raft came crashing down in a spray
of icy droplets.

Elenna sat up, blinking. Her hair
was plastered to her face, but she
had the end of the rope. She grabbed
an arrow from her quiver and started

to tie the rope to one end.

"An anchor!" Tom said with relief. "Good idea!"

Elenna frowned along her arrow, trying to aim at a tree on the shoreline, but her arm wavered with every bump of the raft. The trees were whooshing past so fast Tom couldn't see how she would hit one. Beside them, Silver let out a low growl. The wolf was staring ahead, his fur bristling and his ears flat.

Tom followed Silver's gaze, and a shock of cold fear washed through him. Just ahead, the river turned to raging white froth, then vanished over a ledge.

"Elenna!" Tom cried, seeing the sharp drop speeding ever closer towards them. "Quickly!"

He heard a *whoosh*, followed by a *thunk*, and turned to see the arrow embedded in the trunk of a tree. The rope went taut, and the raft jerked to a stop right at the lip of the falls. Water flowed rapidly around the raft.

"We have to get off!" Elenna cried. "My arrow won't hold long."

Tom glanced towards the shore. It was too far to jump. He grabbed his shield and plunged it into the water. Drawing on the power of his Golden Armour, he paddled them in, muscles straining as he forced his shield through the foaming river.

Just as he thought his strength would fail, Elenna leaned out of the raft and grabbed a straggly bush.

"Got it!" she said, helping to pull them in to shore.

Elenna led Storm to the bank. Tom went next, beckoning Silver to follow them.

The wolf was crouched, ready to leap, when Tom heard a sickening *twang*. The arrow anchoring the raft had pulled free.

"No!" Elenna cried. Tom reached hopelessly towards Silver as the raft was snatched away by the current. Silver's paws scrabbled on the wood. Elenna screamed in horror. With a terrible, anguished howl, the wolf vanished over the falls.

"Silver!" Elenna cried, clambering over rocks towards the cliff-edge. Tom scrambled after her. When he

reached the edge, he looked down.
It was a sheer drop, craggy with
rocks, ending in a pool of foaming
water. Their raft was spinning in the
shallows, a splintered gash along one
side. Silver was nowhere to be seen.

Tom felt sick and numb as he

stared at the deadly drop. Tears flowed down Elenna's cheeks. Tom put his hand on her shoulder. Her body was shuddering with sobs.

"He might have made it," Tom said, trying to believe his words. "We will get down. If Silver's alive, we will find him."

Elenna wiped her nose with her sleeve and nodded.

Slowly and in silence, they led Storm along the edge of the ravine until they found a path he could follow.

When they reached the bottom, Elenna's face was pale.

"He's not here," she said. "I thought maybe…" She trailed off, and took a shuddering breath. Tom could feel his own throat aching with tears. He swallowed hard.

"There's still hope," he said.

"We should keep on with the Quest," Elenna said. "Silver wouldn't want us to stop."

Tom glanced towards their raft, adrift in the pool. Two planks had split away, but the rest looked largely undamaged.

"I think the raft will still hold us," Tom said. "And from the map it looked as if the river would take us to the next Treasure. The water runs more smoothly from here. It's possible Silver was washed downstream. We'll look for him on the way." Elenna nodded, but Tom could see she was distraught.

Tom made his way to the pool, and fished a plank from the raft out of the water. He hacked it into two pieces with his sword and handed one half to Elenna.

"We can use these as paddles," Tom said. He waded into the water's edge and retrieved the remains of the raft, then tugged it to shore.

Elenna led Storm aboard, then sank down beside him. Her red-rimmed eyes looked fierce.

"Rotu had better keep out of my way!" she said.

Tom stepped on beside her and sat down. As they drifted back out into the current, he dipped his paddle.

The tumbling roar of the falls

became a soft rush as they slid downriver. Soon, the only sounds Tom could hear were the splash of their paddles and the wind in the trees. He glanced about, checking the riverbanks for any patch of grey.

His mind felt heavy and dull with grief. He couldn't see how Silver would have survived.

He shook himself, and started to row with determined strokes. *We have a deadly Beast to defeat and a war to stop. Our duty is to the Quest.*

4

FANGS IN THE MIST

As they rowed, the landscape flattened out and the river grew wide and sluggish. Thick grey clouds hung low overhead.

Soon the river branched into small streams that flowed into boggy fields. Rows of short green stalks poked up. Tom spotted raised banks of earth among them.

"Rice paddies," he said, pointing.

"This land is farmed."

Elenna scanned the wind-blasted fields. "So where are the workers?"

Tom shrugged. "Maybe something scared them away."

As they went on past the deserted paddy fields, banks of clinging mist drifted across the river.

Tom peered ahead. Soon he could make out the shadowy forms of buildings on stilts.

He nudged Elenna. "That must be where the farmers live."

The huts were part of a small village on the bank, shrouded in mist and as silent as a boneyard. *The houses must be on stilts in case the river floods*, Tom realised.

"There!" Elenna said, indicating a

window. Tom glimpsed the pale face of a child before it quickly darted out of sight.

"They're afraid," Tom said. "We're in the right place."

They rowed their raft towards a muddy bank and clambered off. As Tom led Storm onto dry land, his limbs felt terribly heavy with exhaustion and grief.

"Hello," he called up towards the ghostly buildings. "We come in peace." Tom heard nothing but the slap of water on wood.

Suddenly a sharp yelp of fear cut through the mist, followed by a long, low moan. It seemed to be coming from a house nearby.

"Stay here," Tom said, laying a hand on his horse's flank. Tom and Elenna climbed rickety stairs up to the door of the house. Tom knocked.

"Leave us be!" said a gruff voice.

"We've come from Pania to try to help," Tom called. "Please, let us talk to you."

He heard frightened voices, then the sound of a bolt being drawn. *Only a Beast could cause this much terror*, Tom thought. The door swung open, revealing a slight man with grey hair and worried eyes.

"From Pania, you say?" the man asked, glancing at their weapons.

Tom nodded.

"Then you'd better come in." The

man turned, and Tom and Elenna
followed him into the hut.

The dim room was lit only by a
smoking fire. At the back, a woman
with grey plaits sat beside a low
bed. As Tom approached it, he saw
a young man under the rumpled

blankets, staring about himself with wild eyes.

"It'll eat us alive!" the young man whimpered, shrinking back against the wall. "And it's all my fault!"

"Hush, son," the woman cooed. As she stroked the young man's hair, Tom saw his face was covered in scratches and angry red welts, like rope burns.

"What happened?" Tom asked.

"He went out yesterday to work in the paddies," the old man said. "Came back last night like this. All he talks about is a monster trying to eat him."

"It will kill us all!" the youth cried.

"Hush, Brennan, hush," the woman said, dashing a tear from her eyes.

"He's talking about a Beast," Elenna said.

The old man nodded. "The monster of the marshes. It's a fireside tale we tell the children. Poor Brennan's now got the whole village too terrified to go out."

"May I talk to him?" Tom asked. "I've seen this before."

The woman glanced at her cowering son. "If you think you can help," she said.

Tom knelt at the young man's side.

"Brennan," Tom said. "Can you tell me what happened?"

The young man turned towards Tom, but his eyes were wide and blank.

"Can you tell us about the Beast?"

Elenna asked.

"It had teeth!" The young man
shivered as he spoke. "The man told
it to eat me. I shouldn't have tried
to cheat him. I should…" Brennan's
whole body trembled. He whimpered
and flinched away. "I didn't mean

it!" he cried, his forehead creased in anguish. His mother grabbed his hand and squeezed it. Brennan fell back against his pillows, his eyes rolling up under their lids.

Suddenly, a chorus of cries rang out. "The monster!" someone shouted. "It's here!"

Tom and Elenna dashed from the hut, and down the steps to the path. Storm trotted over to them.

"That way!" a man cried from the riverbank, pointing out into the misty fields. The villagers had gathered, holding torches, clubs and sharp-looking scythes.

Tom gestured to Storm to wait, then struck off along a raised path threading between the flooded paddies with Elenna at his side. They crept through the dank fog, listening. All Tom could hear was their footsteps, and the frightened mutters from the townsfolk behind them. He could hardly see a thing. Suddenly a throaty growl echoed around them.

Elenna took a sharp breath, and Tom drew his sword. The growling became an angry rumble. Tom turned about, trying to find the source.

"Look!" Elenna pointed. There was a shape in the shifting mist about thirty paces away. It moved effortlessly over the flooded field.

The growling erupted into a frenzy of snarling. The mist rolled in and the strange shape vanished again.

"We've got it!" came a cry from

over by the riverbank. Tom ran towards the voice.

Soon he could make out the shadowy outlines of people, and something else, writhing on the ground. The shapes became clearer, and Tom could see two men holding a net. The creature inside was a mess of wet fur, white fangs and angry yellow eyes. It was snarling madly.

Elenna gasped and rushed forwards. "Silver!" she cried.

5

KILL THE BEAST

"Keep back!" one of the men holding the net cried. "This monster is dangerous!"

"He's not a monster," Elenna said, smiling through tears. "He's my friend. His name's Silver."

The net bulged and the men holding it staggered as Silver struggled to reach Elenna.

"Please let him go," Tom said,

stepping forward. "I promise he'll do you no harm."

"Keep back!" the man shouted again, as Silver twisted and writhed. "Brennan was right. The marsh monster's real. It must be destroyed."

"No!" Elenna cried.

"You can't!" Tom said. He lunged for the net, but a man stepped forward, swinging his club.

Thud! Red light flashed before Tom's eyes as his skull exploded with pain. He tried to stay upright, but his legs folded under him, and he sank into darkness.

When Tom awoke, he could hear voices in the distance. He was lying

on greasy planks of wood, his hands
bound before him. His head was
throbbing. Tom opened his eyes
cautiously, making out the houses
raised on stilts.

We're back at the village.

He pushed himself onto his elbows
and saw that he was at the back
of the jetty that jutted out over
the river. Elenna lay unconscious
beside him, her hands tied too. Tom
clenched his jaw against the anger
and pain.

"Kill it! Kill it!" The distant voices
rose in a chant.

"Elenna!" Tom hissed. "Wake up!"
Elenna's eyes flickered open.

"Silver!" she mumbled.

"Kill it!" The chanting was getting

louder by the second. Tom saw a group of people wading towards them through the fields. They carried a bundle the size of a wolf held above their heads. The procession stopped on the jetty next to a tall wooden frame. They heaved Silver to the ground and dragged him roughly from the net. One man pulled out a rope and started tying a loop.

"Kill it! Kill it!" the villagers cried.

"We have to stop them," Elenna said, tugging at the ropes tied around her wrists.

Tom remembered his golden breastplate. *If I can just focus...* He shifted his attention to the rope on his wrists, and felt the power of the chainmail flow through him. He

could feel the rope stretching, its
sinews beginning to snap one by one.
But it was so slow!

Tom glanced towards the jetty.
There was a rope around Silver's
neck. One of the men was passing

the other end over the beam of a makeshift scaffold. Panic seared through Tom. *Oh no... They're stringing him up!*

Elenna let out a cry. "Stop! Don't hurt him!"

A thickset man pulled down on the rope, lifting Silver from the ground by his neck. The wolf was silent, but his legs kicked as he rose into the air.

"Stop!" Elenna screamed. But Silver rose higher and the shouts for his blood went on. There was another sound as well. A deep, thudding vibration. *Hoofbeats!*

Suddenly Storm burst through the fog and surged towards the jetty. Cries of panic went up from the crowd as the stallion charged into their midst. His hooves came crashing down onto the deadly scaffolding.

Storm let out a whinny of rage as the scaffolding toppled. Silver tumbled onto the jetty, and the people around him scattered, crying out with fear.

"Silver! Here!" Elenna called. Silver shook out his muddy coat, then bounded towards Tom and Elenna, followed by Storm.

Silver licked away Elenna's tears, then dropped his muzzle to the ropes at her wrists. His sharp teeth sliced through her bonds, then Tom's. Tom scrambled to his feet. Through the fog, he could see people rushing towards them.

"Stop the monster!" they cried.

Elenna was on her knees, her arms around Silver's neck. Storm was stamping and blowing angrily, as Tom tried to soothe him. Soon they were surrounded. Townsfolk of all ages, even children, stared at them with hostility.

Tom stepped forward. "This wolf is not your monster," he said. "He's our friend. You're still in danger from the Beast that attacked Brennan. We came here to defeat it."

"Why should we believe you?" a gruff voice shouted. Murmurs of agreement spread among the villagers. Before Tom could answer, a young girl's piping voice came from the back of the crowd.

"There's something in the fields!"
she cried, tugging desperately at her
mother's hand.

"Hush!" her mother said. "There's
nothing out there but mist."

"I saw it!" the child whimpered.
"It's big as our house. It's coming!"

Tom stared into the mist. He could
hear a strange squelching and
slithering. And there was a smell…a
putrid, rotten smell that made his
stomach turn. A huge, gangly shape
rose up out of the mud ahead.

Out of instinct, Tom reached
for his sword, but it wasn't there.
"Where are our weapons?" he
demanded.

"Why should we tell you?" said one of the villagers.

"Because the real monster is coming!" said Elenna. "And we're the only ones who can fight it."

But the Beast had vanished again.

"It must be scared," said a villager. A sudden scream made everyone turn around. At the back of the crowd, a thick, sinuous tendril had wrapped around the girl's ankle. *It's circled around us!* Tom thought.

"Lettie!" the girl's mother cried as the Beast yanked her daughter from her grip.

Tom leapt after the tiny figure, her mother's screams ringing in his ears. He pounded over the ground

as the child disappeared into the
river, held tight in the Beast's
deadly grasp.

THE SNAPPING MAW

"Someone help her!" shrieked the girl's mother.

I won't let her perish! Tom thought. He dived off the jetty into icy water filled with thrashing roots. He lunged for one and grabbed hold. Pricks of pain erupted in his hands as thorns dug into his flesh. Tom held the root

tighter. Suddenly, it was gripping
him back, wrapping about his
wrist. Another tendril snatched at
his waist. Tom felt a rush of speed
as he was plucked from the water
and slammed into the soft mud of

the opposite riverbank. He heard
a scream beside him, and saw the
little girl struggling on the muddy
bank, wrapped in a thorny limb.

"Tom!" Elenna cried.

Tom twisted in the Beast's grasp

and looked back at the jetty. He
could barely see Elenna through the
mist. *She can't fire her bow without
a clear shot!*

From above him came a strange
creaking sound which could only be
Beastly laughter.

Tom looked up to see the Beast's
waxy petals hanging open in a
jagged-toothed grin. Inside its
gaping mouth were several goggling
eyes. They were all swivelled down
towards him.

Tom felt a stab of revulsion. *It can
watch its victims as it eats them!* He
swallowed his disgust. Behind the
eyes, deep in the creature's throat, he

could see a circle of gleaming gold. *The queen's ring!*

A thin wail cut the air, and Tom looked up to see the little girl's feet kicking frantically as she was lifted towards the Beast's mouth.

No, you don't! Tom plunged his sword, point downwards, into the limb that held him. The tendril jerked, hurling Tom through the air. He came down with a jarring splash in the shallows at the river's edge, not far from the jetty. He scrambled up. The little girl screamed again. The Beast was opening its jaws wider, the eyes inside bulging as they watched the struggling child. Horror gripped hold of Tom. *I have to save her, but how?*

Thwack! An arrow thudded into
the coil that held the girl. Tom
glanced at the jetty, relief flooding
though him. *Elenna!* He could see
his friend clearly, standing ankle-
deep in water. Her bow was raised
for another shot. *Thud!* Her second
shot landed beside her first. The
Beast's injured tendril sprang open,
flinging the screaming girl back
across the river. Tom scrambled
through the mud, snatched up the
child and ran.

He could hear the Beast's jaws
chattering in rage behind him. He
heaved the girl higher onto his
shoulder and scrambled towards
the wooden jetty.

Elenna fired again, and Tom

looked over his shoulder to see the Beast's limbs recoil. Another arrow bit into the creature's waxy flower. The Beast gnashed its teeth in fury then turned and slunk back into the water. Soon nothing was left but ripples on the surface and a lingering, putrid stench.

Tom carried the shivering girl to the jetty, where her mother grabbed her, sobbing breathlessly.

The thickset man who had captured Silver put his hand out towards Tom.

"We are in your debt," he said. "Sorry we didn't trust you."

Tom shook the outstretched hand,

and smiled grimly. "It's not over yet," he said. "The Beast will return. I need to talk to Brennan and find out everything I can."

"There are stables near Brennan's hut," the man said. "You're welcome to house your animals there. I'll let Brennan know you are coming." The man turned and left. The rest of the villagers were hurrying away too, talking in hushed and frightened voices. Tom heard doors slamming as they reached their huts.

He and Elenna led Storm and Silver through the village to an empty, run-down stable, before heading back to Brennan's hut.

As soon as they stepped inside, they could see Brennan was feeling better. He was sitting up in bed, sipping from a mug. His mother was on a chair beside him. She rose and beckoned for Tom and Elenna to take her place.

Tom sat. "Tell us everything, from the beginning," he said. "We need to find out more about this Beast – we've never faced one like it."

Brennan told Tom and Elenna about the stranger. How he had given Brennan the ring to sell, then thanked him for delivering it to the Beast.

Elenna shook her head in disgust. "Velmal!" she said. "He was too cowardly to give the Beast the ring himself, so he tricked Brennan."

Brennan looked down at his blankets. "I tried to trick him too," he said. "I suppose I learned my lesson. He wanted me to be the Beast's meal – I was fortunate to escape alive."

Tom turned to Elenna. "I saw the ring in the Beast's throat," he said. "Somehow we have to get it out without killing the Beast."

Elenna grimaced. "It's not going to be easy," she said. "We'd better go."

When they stepped from the hut, dusk was falling. Tom looked out across the shallow waters of the paddies. Beneath the silent blanket of mist, he knew the Beast was lurking. There was no time to lose.

We need to get those Treasures back to Pania.

Elenna seemed to read his thoughts, and gave him a grim nod. They struck off into the fields. Cold water sloshed about Tom's shins as he pressed forwards into the gloom.

A tremor ran through the water. There was a squelching, bubbling sound, and Tom caught a whiff of a familiar choking stench.

"It's coming!" Tom said.

Elenna grabbed his arm and pointed. Ahead of them, the water seemed to boil. Suddenly the Beast's putrid flower shot up from the boggy field and climbed into the sky, towering above them. Its waxy petals snapped open.

Bulging eyes stared at Tom from
between grinning yellow teeth. Tom
put a hand to the red jewel in his
belt, and heard the Beast's voice

boom in his head.

"I am Xerik the Bone Cruncher!" the Beast cried, its roots whipping around it. "No human will ever master me!"

Tom drew his sword, and lifted it high. "We'll see about that!" he said.

WILDFIRE

Tom circled the Beast, looking for a way through its thrashing limbs. The Beast's eyes followed him, staring out from between its jaws.

Elenna lifted her bow and fired. Her arrow sank into a tendril. A shudder ran through the Beast and its goggling eyes swivelled, turning towards her.

"Watch out!" Tom cried, as a root

flickered under the surface of the
water. Elenna jumped back, and
Tom lunged and sliced. His sword
glanced off the tendril, leaving a
pale gash. It flashed past him and
coiled around Elenna's ankle.

"Ah!" Elenna yelped as the Beast yanked her off her feet and hurled her into the mud. Xerik's staring eyes snapped back towards Tom.

A root shot towards him through the air. Tom lifted his shield and caught the blow, staggering under its power. Another root stabbed for his face. He swung his sword and smashed it away, but more were slicing towards him. Tom ducked and spun, blocking with his shield and swiping with his sword.

Something grabbed his shoulder. Tom turned, swinging his sword.

"Whoa!" Elenna cried. Tom lowered his blade with relief at the sight of his friend, but another tendril darted towards them. Elenna's bow twanged. The writhing limb sprang away, an arrow stuck in its flesh.

Tom felt thorns dig into his ankle. He stabbed downwards, sinking his sword deep into the Beast's flesh. Air hissed angrily through Xerik's teeth and he wrenched his tendril away, almost pulling Tom from his feet. Tom caught his balance but another of the Beast's snaking limbs was already flickering towards him. Tom smashed it aside.

This is hopeless! He could feel his muscles tiring, and the chill of the water seeping through him as he cut and thrust. Elenna's bow sang as she fired arrow after arrow, but Xerik wasn't slowing.

A heavy blow smashed into the back of Tom's knees. He fell backwards into cold mud with a cry. He tried to scrabble up, but his hands and feet skidded. A root snagged about his ankle. Another tendril twisted around his sword and flung it away.

Elenna let out a cry of pain, and tumbled into the mud beside him. Anger and frustration flared inside Tom. He kicked hard and wrenched his leg free from the root.

This isn't working! Tom thought. *I need to get in closer, somehow. Maybe if I climb it…*

Suddenly, he heard the splashing coming towards him. Xerik's roots recoiled back from Tom as the Beast craned its stem toward the sound.

Tom saw a rider come to a stop, holding a flaming torch above his head. Tom recognised him at once. *Rotu!* The prince swung his torch about, making Xerik's shadow dance menacingly.

The Beast grinned, tendrils shimmering in the torchlight as they glided towards the prince, astride his horse. Tom leapt to his feet and grabbed his sword.

"Die, vile Beast!" Rotu cried, thrusting his torch down against one of Xerik's roots.

Orange flames licked up Xerik's limb. The Beast rolled its eyes and snatched the burning tendril away. Sparks flew as the limb flicked

through the air, and more roots
crackled into flame. The Beast's
teeth chattered. It writhed in pain.
Tom could hear the pop and crackle
of burning sap. The air filled with
acrid smoke and glowing sparks as
flames engulfed Xerik's flower.

A great shudder ran through
the Beast. Its eyes opened wide.
Suddenly, it toppled, crashing down
into the muddy water. Clouds of
black smoke billowed up, and flakes
of soot rained down as the Beast
disappeared under the mud.

Tom peered into the smoke, looking
for any sign of Xerik. All he could
see was the prince grinning at
his victory, his eyes shining in the
torchlight.

Tom felt a cold dread settle deep in
his bones. *If the Beast is destroyed*,
Tom thought, *the queen's ring will be
lost forever.*

Then another thought hit him.

If Xerik is dead, I have broken my oath as Master of the Beasts.

Tom hung his head in shame. The Quest was over.

I've failed.

8

XERIK'S REVENGE

Prince Rotu swung his horse round.

Tom glared up at him angrily. "Have you any idea what you've done?" he shouted.

"Saved your skin?" Rotu answered, curling his lip in a sneer.

Elenna stormed towards him. "What did you think you were doing when you cut that rope back at the river?" she cried. "You almost got us killed. We thought Silver was dead!"

The prince frowned and shrugged. "It was a joke," he said.

Elenna balled her fists. "A joke!" she shouted. "You –"

Tom put his hand on Elenna's shoulder. She spun around, her face red with anger.

The prince dug his heels into his horse's sides and cantered away. Tom watched, seething with anger too.

Elenna kicked up muddy water as the hoofbeats faded into silence. "I suppose he thinks he's the hero now, for defeating Xerik!" she said.

Tom shook his head. "He thinks it's a game, but if Avantia and Tangala go to war now the ring is lost, his meddling could cost him dearly."

"It will cost his people more,"
Elenna said. "But I don't expect that
he cares!"

Tom and Elenna trudged back to
the village. Tom felt exhausted
and defeated. The mist had cleared
and a waxing moon shone brightly
between tattered clouds, but it didn't
cheer his mood. As they passed
Brennan's hut, Tom heard chattering.
Brennan threw open the door. His
eyes shone and his cheeks were red.

"Come in!" he called. "We're
celebrating the prince's victory over
the Beast."

Tom heard the smug voice of Rotu
waft through the open doorway. "As

soon as I saw that Beast," the prince was saying, "I knew that fire would be its enemy!"

Tom shook his head at Brennan. He wasn't sure how he would react coming face to face with Rotu again.

"Suit yourself," Brennan said, looking a little disappointed, before going inside.

Tom heard the room erupt with laughter, and felt anger welling inside him once again. He took a breath of cool night air, and started towards the stables with Elenna at his side. The sound of Rotu's voice drifted after them.

"Wardok the Sky Terror was even more deadly than Xerik," Rotu was saying. "But he was no match for me.

I ran him into a cliff."

"Rotu's a fool and a liar," Tom said. "I wish he'd stay out of our way! He's ruined our chances of saving the king's marriage."

Elenna sighed. "There are still two more Beasts," she said. "We need to defeat them to protect the kingdom of Tangala. Maybe if we return most of the jewels, the queen will believe we're innocent."

Tom felt a flicker of hope. "You're right," he said. "Let's leave Rotu to brag, and save what we still can of this Quest."

As they stepped into the musty dimness of the stables, Silver padded towards them and slipped his nose into Elenna's hand. "You look so much stronger!" Elenna said.

Storm whickered softly and Tom ran a hand along his stallion's coat. Elenna bent and Silver gently licked her face. Tom felt his anger draining away. *Things could have been so much worse...*

Suddenly the ground beneath their feet shuddered. Silver growled and Elenna sprang up as dust floated down from the ceiling. *An earthquake?*

Outside a loud crack echoed through the night, followed by cries of alarm. Tom and Elenna darted for the door. Terrified screams were coming from the direction of Brennan's hut.

Tom looked, and felt a surge of

adrenaline. *The Beast lives!* Towering over the hut, Tom could see Xerik's gnarled, sinewy form, charred limbs writhing in the moonlight. The hut was leaning at a horrible angle, and villagers were pouring down its slanting steps.

Xerik's eyes were glinting angrily.

Tom dashed towards the hut. Xerik's long, powerful tendrils tugged at the stilts that held it up. The hut creaked as the stilts toppled and fell. It crashed down into the mud, its stairs splintering beneath it. Tom scanned the retreating villagers, looking for Rotu.

"Help!" he heard Rotu cry.

That fool of a prince is still inside

the hut! Tom realised. He dashed
forward. A tendril snapped down
in front of him, blocking his way. It
glided past him, through the tilted
doorway. From inside, the prince let
out a terrified scream.

Tom slashed at the root, but his sword glanced off Xerik's charred and blackened flesh. The tendril whipped back through the door, dragging the prince out with it. Rotu reached towards Tom, his eyes wide with terror. Tom lunged, trying to catch hold of Rotu's arms, but Xerik's limb snatched the prince away. The Beast gave Tom a hideous grin, then turned and crawled towards the river.

Tom tore after the Beast, his feet pounding over the ground. Silver raced beside him, snarling. Elenna's bow twanged, and an arrow whizzed past. The shot hit the jetty with a thud as Xerik plunged into the river, dragging the prince in with him.

Tom skidded to a stop. The prince's screams echoed across the water and Xerik's flailing limbs kicked up foamy waves. Silver prowled along the jetty, growling.

I can't hope to defeat Xerik in the river, Tom thought. *There has to be another way!* Then he noticed the rope that had been used to string up Silver still lying in a heap on the wooden planks.

He turned to Elenna. "I'm going to drag Xerik out," he said.

Elenna frowned. "How?"

Tom dashed forward and grabbed the rope. "Get Storm!" he called back to her.

"Tom! Wait!" Elenna cried.

But there was no time to lose. Tom bent his knees and dived neatly off the jetty.

SETTING THE TRAP

The icy chill of the water took Tom's breath away, but he looped the rope over his shoulder and swam. Xerik's limbs were thrashing wildly as he tried to seize the prince. Rotu's legs were braced against Xerik's waxy petals, and he waved his sword.

Just stay alive! Tom thought. He took a deep breath and dived under the water, kicking forward powerfully.

Soon a black snaking shape loomed before him in the gloom. *A root!* And there was another. Tom was surrounded by Xerik's thorny limbs. He kicked his legs, forcing himself downwards, then shrugged the rope from his shoulder. Carefully, Tom

swam between Xerik's limbs, draping loops of rope around each one. When he judged he had just enough rope left, he turned to swim back to shore.

With the last of his strength, he pushed towards the deeper darkness of the bank. When he reached it, he shot up out of the water, gasping.

"Tom!" Elenna cried. "I was worried you'd drowned!" Tom grabbed her hand and scrambled onto the bank where Storm and Silver were waiting. The villagers were huddled at a distance, watching. A woman slapped a hand over her mouth and pointed.

"Help! Get it off me!" Rotu cried. A thick tendril was wrapped around the prince's neck. Rotu gave a strangled gulp then went silent. Elenna fired

her bow. An arrow hit Xerik's stem.
The Beast shook his head in fury but
didn't loosen his grip on the prince.

Tom turned to Storm. "I need your
help," he said. The stallion tossed his
mane, and Tom wrapped the rope
around his chest to make a harness.

"Pull!" Tom cried, slapping Storm's
flank. Storm lifted his head and
whinnied, heaving with all his might.
But the stallion's hooves slipped. Tom
braced himself against Storm's rump.
He pushed hard, calling on the power
of his Golden Armour. Storm's hooves
bit into the ground and the stallion
leapt forwards. Xerik's stem juddered.
His limbs writhed as he toppled and
crashed into the water, taking the
prince down with him.

"Pull!" Tom cried again.

Storm's breath snorted from his nostrils and his muscles strained as he inched up the bank. Xerik's head rose from the water near the shore, and his teeth chattered in rage.

Elenna ran behind Storm and helped the push. Storm's muscles bunched and heaved.

"Almost there!" Tom said.

Storm lowered his head, braced his feet and gave one last, mighty tug. Xerik's roots flailed in the slimy mud, trying to find a grip, but there was nothing to hold. The Beast slid, muddy and dripping, onto the bank.

Tom spotted the prince, still grasped in Xerik's root.

"Rotu! Here!" Elenna cried.

Tom lunged forwards and hacked at the root that held the prince. Elenna heaved Rotu to safety.

SNAP! Xerik rose up suddenly, and Storm tumbled forwards, the frayed end of the rope swinging free.

Oh no! It's broken!

All at once, snaking roots surrounded Tom. Xerik's creaking laughter rang out around him. Suddenly he felt a root around his neck. Thorns bit into his skin as the coil closed tight. The blood pounded in his temples and he gasped for breath. He tried to cry for help, but his voice came out as a croak. Another limb swooped down and curled about his wrist.

More roots grabbed his ankles. Tom

struggled frantically but couldn't
move. He couldn't breathe. Then
Xerik started to pull. Tom felt his
limbs tugged in opposite directions.
His legs burned in agony at the strain.
The pain was tremendous. Bright
specks swam before his eyes and

blackness swallowed the edges of his vision. *I'm passing out!* Tom felt a surge of panic. His vision began to fade. *This is it*, he thought. *It's over*.

But then, through the blackness, he heard a familiar *twang*.

Elenna's bow! A flicker of hope kindled inside him. He felt a jolt run through the limb that gripped his neck. Suddenly the pressure was gone. Tom gasped, desperately sucking in air. As the darkness receded he felt his strength returning. He turned and saw one of Elenna's arrows pinning Xerik's tendril to the ground. Tom thanked his luck for his friend's sharp shooting.

Elenna fired more arrows. Each shot thudded into the end of a flailing root, pinning it down. Tom's sword arm sprang free. He lifted the blade and cut straight through the root about his ankle, tumbling from Xerik's grasp. Silver snarled, snapping at roots, and Storm stamped, crushing them under his hooves.

Xerik's thick stem twisted as he tried to escape Elenna's arrows. Soon just a single root was left free, snaking across the ground.

Elenna stood her ground and fired. *Thwack!* The root was pinned to the ground. Xerik was defenceless. The creature's head weaved from side to side as he struggled against his bonds.

Tom scrambled to his feet and frowned up at the Beast. Xerik's gaping maw snapped open and his eyes stared down at Tom. He rested his hand on the red jewel in his belt and heard the Beast roaring in fury.

Tom lifted his sword. "Give me the ring," he said. The Beast bent its head lower. Its eyes were red with fury.

NO! came its voice in Tom's head.

Tom held out his hand. "You are defeated. Give it to me," he said.

I'll swallow you and watch the flesh melt from your bones! Xerik boomed.

At that moment, Tom heard a crack. One of Xerik's massive roots swung upwards, Elenna's arrow still embedded in its flesh. Xerik let out a triumphant cry and sent the pointed tip of the root stabbing towards Tom.

If that's how you want to play it... Tom flung his sword aside and rolled. The root smashed down behind him. Xerik screamed with fury. Tom called on the power of his magic boots, and leapt forward. The Beast's eyes bulged as Tom thrust his shield between its teeth, jamming its jaws wide open. Tom took a breath, and dived in.

ONE FINAL MEAL

Tom was wedged head first in the vile creature's mouth. The stench of Xerik's breath made his eyes water.

There was hardly room to move but Tom forced himself downwards into the Beast's throat. Xerik's eyes twisted towards him as he squirmed past. Muscular walls of flesh closed around him. Tom could feel them trying to suck his body down.

The skin on his hands and face was stinging where Xerik's slime had touched, and his eyes were starting to burn. He stared down into the darkness of the creature's guts where he could see a faint glimmer.

He blinked again, trying to focus.

Yes! The queen's ring gleamed deep in Xerik's throat. Tom heaved himself onwards, bracing his knees to stop the Beast swallowing him.

He reached out his hand, almost touching the ring. There was a bubbling sound and a belch of vile green gas erupted in Tom's face. His stomach churned, but he fought back his sickness and reached further.

SNAP! Suddenly everything went dark. His shield must have slipped down into Xerik's mouth.

I'm trapped inside the Beast. Tom couldn't see a thing. The suctioning pull of Xerik's mouth increased. A laugh rang out all around him. Tom heard the gurgling bubble of Xerik's stomach, waiting to digest him.

He braced his body against Xerik's throat and reached further and further down. The skin on his face was burning now. *I'm being eaten alive!* At last he felt the cool, smooth lines of the ring. He grasped it.

Tom felt a rush of triumph. *Time to get out of here!* He summoned the power of his golden breastplate, feeling its strength in his muscles.

Now! Tom tucked in his chin and rolled, turning round in the tight space. Then he forced himself up into Xerik's mouth. He braced his back against one slimy side of the Beast's jaws, and pushed hard with his legs against the other. He could feel the great Beast fighting to keep its mouth closed.

"Yah!" Tom cried, giving one final heave of his legs. Xerik's mouth flipped open and Tom leapt out, clutching the ring.

He landed in a pool of slime. Xerik towered over him, its mouth gaping and its round eyes swivelling madly.

Tom met his gaze. "You are defeated," he said, holding up the ring for Xerik to see. As Xerik's eyes rested on the ring, the great Beast sagged. Its root-like limbs sank to the ground and its head hung forwards. Its mouth clacked shut.

Tom scraped the slime from his face with his hands, and got up.

Elenna wrinkled her nose, then grinned at him. Beside her, Rotu was staring at the defeated Beast. Then he lifted his sword with a cry of triumph and dashed towards Xerik.

Silver snarled and leapt forward, grabbing the prince's cloak in his teeth. Rotu's boots skidded, and he slipped into the mud with a splat.

Elenna shook her head in disgust. "Can't you see this Beast is defeated?"

she said. She pointed, and Xerik's slumped form glowed green for a moment, then vanished. The prince frowned in confusion.

The anger that had been growing inside Tom suddenly flared. He rounded on the prince.

"What is wrong with you?" Tom shouted. "You have no idea what a Quest is about! It's time you stopped playing like a spoilt child, and returned to Pania where you belong."

Rotu scrambled up, his face furious. "I saved your life!" he cried.

"You nearly ruined the Quest!" Tom shouted back. "Not everything's about brute force, you know! You're just a bungler, trying to be a warrior, and you aren't ready!"

Rotu's face flushed and his jaw quivered. He shot Tom a look of pure hatred, then turned to stalk away.

Tom felt a pang of remorse as he watched Rotu go.

"Maybe I was too harsh," he said.

"No," Elenna said, "he's a danger to himself and to the Quest. The sooner he's back in Pania the better."

Tom nodded. Elenna was right. But somehow he still felt guilty. He sighed, suddenly exhausted.

"Let's go," he said. "We've got two more Beasts to defeat, and as Daltec said, time is against us."

"Wait!" cried a voice. It was Brennan. "I saw what happened from the village. You were amazing! You must come to our house to recover."

Tom frowned. "I'm sorry, but we don't have time," he said.

"Then take this," Brennan said, drawing a small flask from his pocket. "It's my mother's healing potion, made with rice."

As soon as Tom took a sip he could feel new strength running through him. "Wow!" he said. "This is good!"

"Take it for the journey," Brennan said. "It's the least I can offer. You've given me a second chance."

Tom handed the flask to Elenna, who took a sip too, and they mounted Storm. Tom turned Storm towards the horizon, put his heels to his horse's sides and set off into the wind. They had a Beast to find.

CONGRATULATIONS, YOU HAVE COMPLETED THIS QUEST!

At the end of each chapter you were awarded a special gold coin.
The QUEST in this book was worth an amazing 11 coins.

Look at the Beast Quest totem picture inside the back cover of this book to see how far you've come in your journey to become

MASTER OF THE BEASTS.

The more books you read, the more coins you will collect!

Do you want your own
Beast Quest Totem?

1. Cut out and collect the coin below
2. Go to the Beast Quest website
3. Download and print out your totem
4. Add your coin to the totem
www.beastquest.co.uk/totem

Don't miss the next exciting Beast Quest book, PLEXOR THE RAGING REPTILE!

Read on for a sneak peek...

CHAPTER ONE

THE SEARING DESERT

"Keep going, Storm," said Tom, patting his horse's glistening neck. "We're almost at the oasis." He and Elenna trudged through the searing desert, Tom leading his black stallion by the reins. Even without Tom on his back, Storm was struggling in the heat.

We have to go on. The next Beast must be vanquished.

Silver padded on ahead, his paws leaving deep marks in the fine sand, his tongue lolling from his mouth. Elenna wiped beads of sweat from her forehead as she examined the map of Tangala. Aroha, Queen of this southern land, had told them how the ancient map would lead them to the magical crown jewels which protected the kingdom from Beasts. It was the only clue they had in their Quest to thwart the evil Wizard Velmal. When he had stolen the treasures from the palace in the city of Pania, he had broken the spell which kept the Beasts away.

Tom glanced at the bag that hung from Storm's saddle. Already, he and his companions had managed to defeat two Beasts and take back the crown and the ring. But the orb and the sceptre were still missing.

It was bad enough that Velmal's actions had put the kingdom in peril, but Tom and Elenna were blamed for the theft, threatening to disrupt the planned marriage of King Hugo and Queen Aroha. Without the marriage, the longed-for treaty to restore the union between Avantia and Tangala would be doomed.

Tom knew that the only way he could prove he and Elenna were innocent, and prevent the two kingdoms coming into conflict, was to find the missing jewels and take them back to the Palace.

Read PLEXOR THE RAGING REPTILE to find out more!

FIGHT THE BEASTS, FEAR THE MAGIC

Are you a BEAST QUEST mega fan?
Do you want to know about all the latest news, competitions and books before anyone else?

Then join our Quest Club!

Visit the BEAST QUEST website
and sign up today!

www.beastquest.co.uk

Discover the new Beast Quest mobile game from

MINICLIP
▶ PLAY GAMES

Available free on iOS and Android

  **amazon**.com

Guide Tom on his Quest to free the Good Beasts of
Avantia from Malvel's evil spells.

DOWNLOAD THE APP TO BEGIN
THE ADVENTURE NOW!

UNLOCK YOUR EXCLUSIVE
BEAST QUEST GAME
BATTLE SHIELD

* How to unlock your exclusive shield!

1. Visit www.beast-quest.com/mobilegamesecret

2. Type in the code 2511920

3. Follow the instructions on screen to
reveal your exclusive shield

31901060028299